Don't Dip
Your Chips
in Your Drink, Kate!

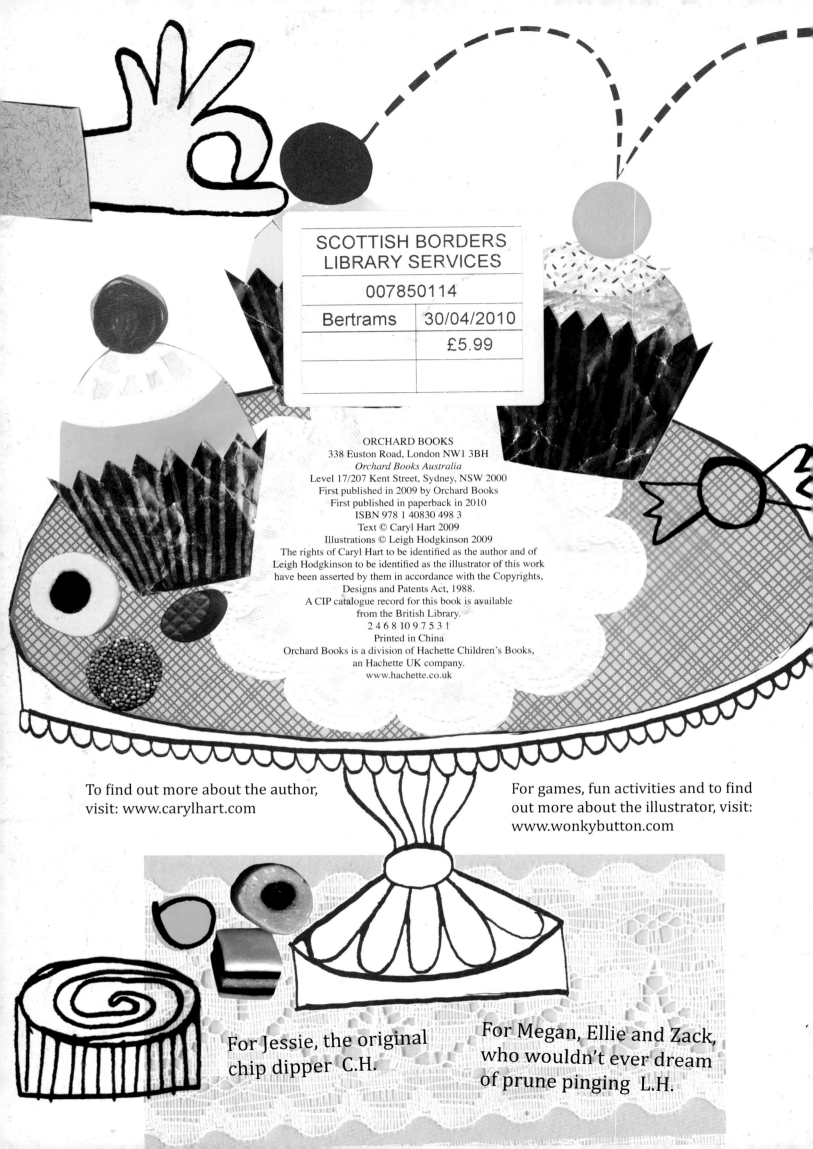

ORCHARD BOOKS
338 Euston Road, London NW1 3BH
Orchard Books Australia
Level 17/207 Kent Street, Sydney, NSW 2000
First published in 2009 by Orchard Books
First published in paperback in 2010
ISBN 978 1 40830 498 3
Text © Caryl Hart 2009
Illustrations © Leigh Hodgkinson 2009
The rights of Caryl Hart to be identified as the author and of
Leigh Hodgkinson to be identified as the illustrator of this work
have been asserted by them in accordance with the Copyrights,
Designs and Patents Act, 1988.
A CIP catalogue record for this book is available
from the British Library.
2 4 6 8 10 9 7 5 3 1
Printed in China
Orchard Books is a division of Hachette Children's Books,
an Hachette UK company.
www.hachette.co.uk

To find out more about the author,
visit: www.carylhart.com

For games, fun activities and to find
out more about the illustrator, visit:
www.wonkybutton.com

For Jessie, the original
chip dipper C.H.

For Megan, Ellie and Zack,
who wouldn't ever dream
of prune pinging L.H.

Don't Dip Your Chips in Your Drink, Kate!

Caryl Hart • Leigh Hodgkinson

ORCHARD BOOKS

"**Don't** dip your chips
in your drink,
Kate!

Eat your cabbage **before** it goes cold.
Don't wipe your nose on your sleeve, Kate.
Why can't you do as you're told?

CHIP SPLat

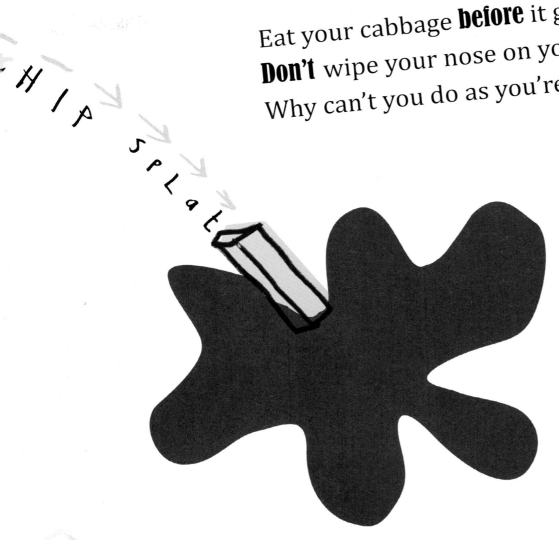

Don't take another potato –
Just eat what you've got on your plate.
Chew your meat, use your fork,
sit still and **don't** talk.
Hurry up or we're going to be late."

Losh

pea whizz

Does your mum tell you off at the table?
Well, mine does it **day** after **day**.
She says I am rude when I mix up my food,
But it tastes so much better that way.

When I tell Fred a joke about **bogies**,
Mum shouts, "Go upstairs straight away.
Don't you dare to come back to the table
Till you've got something **proper** to say."

I flop on my bed feeling grumpy.
Why is Mum being so **mean**?
So, I get out some paper,
a pen and some stamps
And I write a quick note to the *Queen*.

♡ Your Majesty,

could you advise me
About eating AND being ~~good~~ polite?
My mum says I'll NEVER get on in this Life
If I can't get my manners just Right.

Please help me, I'm getting quite
DESPERATE.

I REALLY don't know whAt to do.
Perhaps I can visit Your paLace oNe day
And ~~learn~~ learn to be PoSH
just Like you.

KAteX

A footman arrives the next morning,
with the fanciest letter I've seen.

Miss Kate
P. Green

It has come to Our Royal attention
That you'd like to have tea with the Queen.

Her Majesty would be delighted –
She loves having children to tea.

Dress up smart, don't be late.

Wait by your front gate

Next Thursday

at quarter past three.

The Queen

"You **can't possibly** go," says my mother.
"You'd give Her Royal Highness a fright."

But Fred says, "It's fine.
We've got plenty of time.
Learn these rules
and you should be all right . . ."

THE RULES

NO slurping

NO slouching

NO grabbing

NO burping

DON'T talk with your mouth full of food.

DON'T argue

DON'T shout

DON'T throw things about

DON'T eat with your fingers — it's rude.

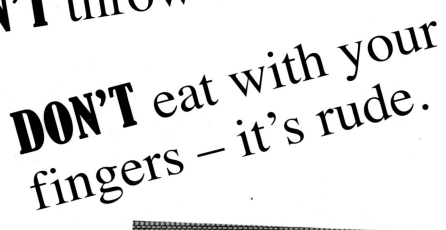

NO yawning

NO whining

NO spitting

NO moaning

DON'T gobble down handfuls of peas.

STAY at the table till told to get down

And **ALWAYS** say thank you and please.

Next Thursday arrives all too quickly.
As a car whisks me off at top speed,
I sink into the seat and try to repeat
All the rules Fred and I have agreed.

What were they?

NO chewing?

NO drinking?

NO talking?

NO thinking?

That **cannot** be right, I am sure.

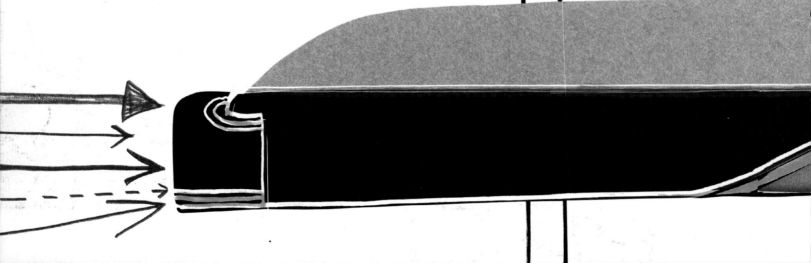

But look!

We've arrived at the palace!
The Queen pulls me
quickly inside.

Then she hurries me down to the kitchen
And flings the fridge door open wide.

"*Good-ee!*" cries the Queen. "*This looks lovely!*"
And she grabs for a tall, wobbly jelly.
She gobbles it down, wipes her hands on her gown,
Then burps and starts rubbing her belly.

She **piles** all the food on the table.
"Pudding first," says the Queen, with a grin.
*"Why don't you start
with that big treacle tart?
Come on now, stuff it all in."*

"Are you sure that's good manners?" I stutter.
"I keep thinking there's something we've missed."
"Oh yes," says the Queen,
"I'll just check the Royal Rules."
And she pulls out a very long list.

Manners for Queens
The Royal Rules

NO slurping

NO slouching

NO grabbing

NO burping

DON'T talk with your mouth full of food.

DON'T argue

DON'T shout

DON'T throw things about

DON'T eat with your fingers — it's rude.

NO yawning
NO whining
NO *spitting*
NO moaning
DON'T *gobble down handfuls of peas.*

STAY at the table till told to get down

And **ALWAYS** *say thank you and please.*

"*Yes, these are the rules we* **should** *stick to . . . . . . but manners are* dull, *don't you think?*"

Then she loads up her spoon
with several dried prunes
And fires them into my drink.

Before I know
what I am doing,
I stick my fork into a bun
And **launch** it
towards Her Royal Highness.

"Forget manners," she cries. *"Let's have fun!"*

We **gobble** down handfuls of cherries
And spit out the stones far and wide.
Then we bite into three dozen doughnuts
And lick out the jam from inside.

We **scoff**
till our tummies are bursting,
Then flop on the sofa to rest.
The Queen says,
*"That dinner was out of this world.
Kate, you are simply*
the best."

So, if your family's **STRICT** about manners,
Even though they can see you're not keen,
Put up a **fight**, show them who's **right**

And send them to tea with the $Queen$.